Text and illustrations:
Copyright © 2017 Aaron Bilgrad
All rights reserved.

ISBN: 978-0-692-89064-690000

Story and Script:
Aaron Bilgrad
The Blank Press
www.TheBlankPress.com

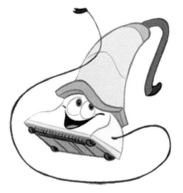

Illustrations, Cover Design, Page Layout:
Zach Wideman, www.widemanillustrations.com

SKYLAR THE VACUUM CLEANER WHO REALLY REALLY REALLY DIDN'T WANT TO GO TO BED

by Aaron Bilgrad

Illustrated by Zach Wideman

She loved it when her family
took her out of the closet
to clean up their mess.

She thought she was so lucky to clean up the broccoli bits, cookie crumbs, and microwavable chicken nuggets that her wonderful family dropped on the floor.

And she loved playing and
dancing with the kids in the house.

She so wanted to keep playing with her toys...

Having fun with the other kids...

And most precious to Skylar...

She wanted to stay up to watch more TV...

Skylar shouted,
"But I want to watch
my favorite show...
Alligator Firefighters!

Her family tried so hard to get her to go to bed.

If there was ever a vacuum cleaner that really
didn't want to go to bed, Skylar was IT!

Skylar really really really
didn't want to go to bed,
and she started crying.

Her tears got all over
the floor, and a frustrated
Martin The Mop had to clean
them up on his day off.

Then her whole family said something important to Skylar, something she had never thought about before. They said, "Skylar, if you get a good night's sleep, then tomorrow you will be the happiest, sharpest, strongest vacuum cleaner you can be!"

And she imagined what a great day tomorrow could be if she was well-rested... She could be her best, most powerful self, and vacuum up everything in the most mighty way!

She could
vacuum dirt from
the kids' shoes...

And Butchy The Cat's kitty litter mess...
that Butchy made on purpose.

And even the stuff that Clarence The New Fancy Vacuum Cleaner was unable to pick up.

Then Skylar the vacuum cleaner put on her pajamas and eagerly got into bed.
Her family tucked her in, and said "Goodnight", and Skylar the vacuum cleaner
had sweet dreams about a wonderful tomorrow.

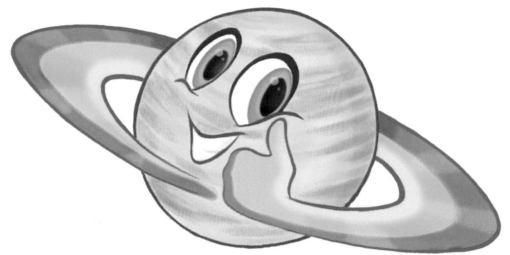

A HappyJoyTime Book

More HappyJoyTime books coming soon!

After graduating from The University of Expensive,

Aaron Bilgrad has researched the emotional needs

and wants of household appliances for over 12 years.

He currently writes books from the inside of a volcano,

despite the lava and high temperature.

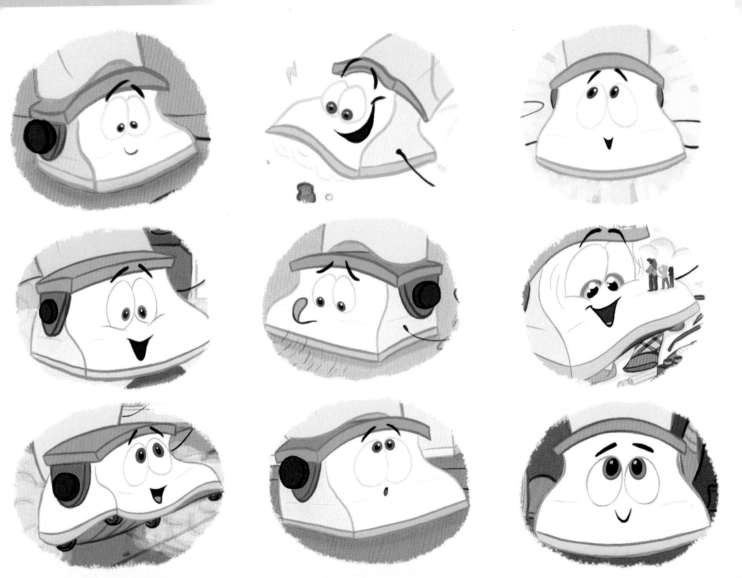